Cecily Cicada

by Kita Helmetag Murdock
and Patsy Helmetag

For Hannah, Evie, Addis and Lucy
"Be patient, dears, and persevere, and never do give up."

Visit us online at cecilycicada.com

In her dreary, earthen hole 'neath the sassafras tree
On Huidekoper Street, in Washington, D.C.,
Lived a hopeful, nymph cicada waiting for the time
She could crawl up top and feel the sunshine.

The last thing she remembered before digging her hole
Was her solemn Mama saying, "Cecily be bold!
Be patient, dear, and persevere, and never do give up,
For in seventeen years you'll get back to the top.

"In seventeen years you'll know what to do,
And something amazing will happen to you!"
For seventeen years she waited day and night
For time and temperature to be just right.

1 Listening

2 Knitting

3 Dancing

4 Drawing

Cecily ate roots, then ate some more,
But eating roots was truly a bore.
So she was stalwart and passed the time
Doing seventeen things that don't fit in this rhyme.

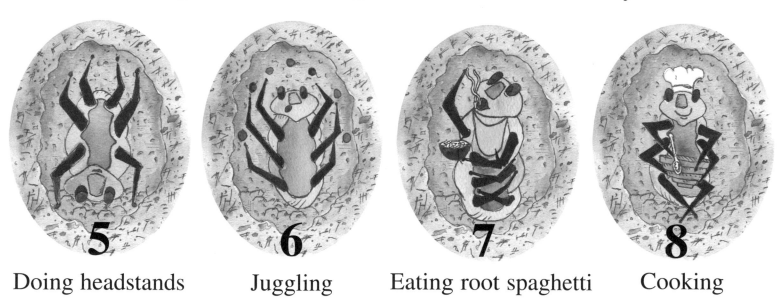

5 Doing headstands

6 Juggling

7 Eating root spaghetti

8 Cooking

9 Making faces

10 Prospecting

11 Reading

12 Singing

17 Sleeping

For while she awaited that far off day,
She had to be clever and learn to play,
And entertain herself 'til the soil felt right.
At sixty-four degrees she could crawl up to the light.

13 Doing Yoga

14 Whistling

15 Throwing a pot

16 Throwing a fit

Once when thinking of things to do,
A friendly worm came passing through.
He said, "Why are you waiting down in this hole?"
She said, "That is something I cannot control.

"In fact, I wish I could go up with you
But I have to wait, my waiting's not through.
For seventeen years I must 'wait the day
When I can come outside and play."

One evening in May she awoke with a start,
This was the moment, she knew in her heart!
Somehow she knew she must go to the top.
She began digging and digging and she did not stop!

Her head popped out in the dim moonlight
But her climbing continued that starry night.
After so many years she felt so free
That she climbed up the bark of that sassafras tree.

When she got near the top she suddenly froze;
She felt stiff from her toes to her nose.
She couldn't move - she was stuck in one spot.
She tried to crawl, and found she could not!

She wiggled and wriggled with all her might,
But no matter what, her feet held tight.
She thought, "I have to get out of here!"
Her body trembled with outright fear!

She began to shake, she couldn't stop shaking,
When all of a sudden she heard something breaking!
She heard a rip, and then a CRACK!
And felt the night air on her back.

She tried moving her feet and found they would.
She took a step and found she could!
But why had she been stuck in one place?
She looked up and saw the dried, brown case.

Her new self was pale with wings that were green,
Her skin was translucent with a beautiful sheen.
When the sun came up on the beings who sleep-in,
Cecily's color began to deepen.

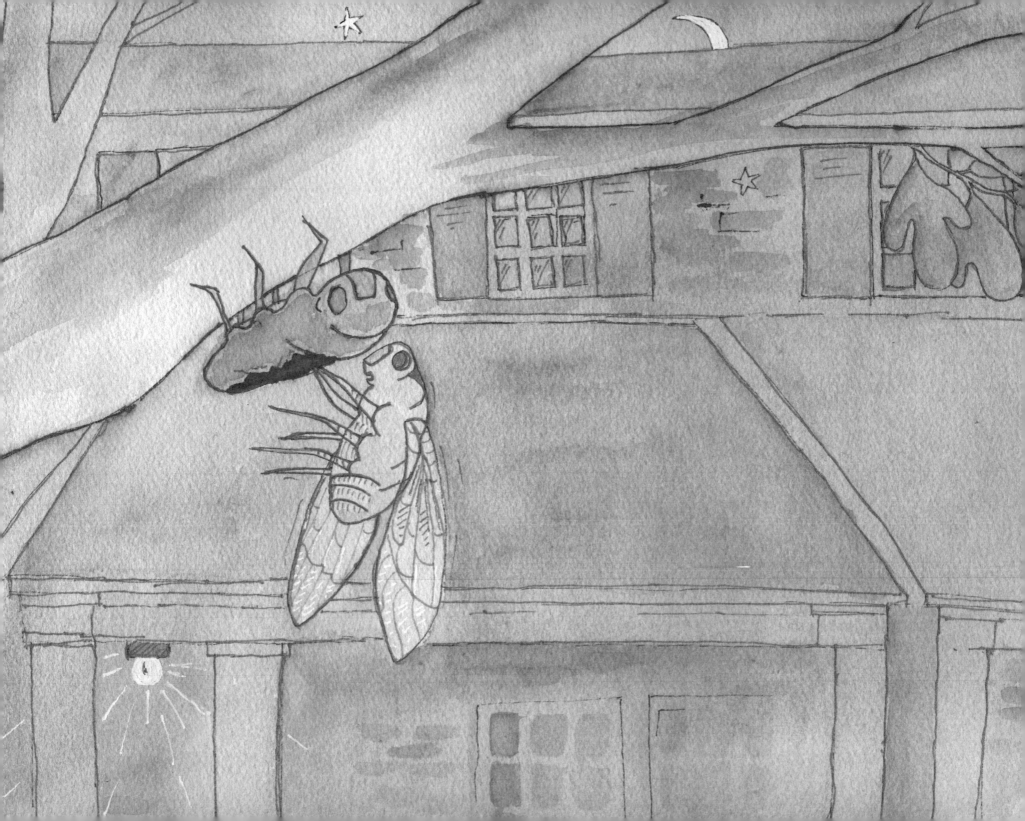

Suddenly a question entered her mind,
"How can I leave part of me behind?
That withered brown case used to be me,
But now it's dried-up and stuck to the tree!"

She saw from her branch a most curious thing,
A creature like she was with elegant wings!
"You look puzzled - but look around,
There are hundreds of us crawling out of the ground!

"Climbing up trees and leaving our past,
Spreading our wings to embrace life at last!
We're leaving our old selves stuck on the trees
While we fly with the ladybugs, robins and bees.

"Oh, it's a wonderful thing to fly!
Jump off the branch. Give it a try!"
It was amazing - her Mom had been right,
As Cecily found on that very first flight.

You know how it is if you've had long to wait.
When that thing finally happens, isn't it great?
If you've been in a dark hole nothing is duller.
Imagine emerging, surrounded by color!

Below her were flowers and beautiful plants,
Birds and dragonflies, spiders and ants.
Children were playing in Glover Park,
And parents were dragging them home before dark,

For two days her red eyes took in all the sights
And the sounds and the smells of springtime delights.
There were savory flowers that smelled so sweet,
And tasty new leaves for her to eat.

Then after three days came a glorious sound
From the bushes and treetops and all around.
From male cicadas both high and low
A chorus of voices began to grow

For some humans it might sound like a buzz
But Cecily knew just what it was -
A beautiful, joyful, thankful song
Of creatures who'd lived in the ground for too long.

Then she heard the sweetest voice,
One that made her heart rejoice.
Cecily looked up and to her surprise
Was another cicada with stars in his eyes.

When you see a cicada please give her a smile
'Cause you may not see one again for a while.
Just look at the grown-up who's reading to you;
When the cicadas come back, you'll be grown up too!

A note from Kita

When I found out that the seventeen-year cicadas were coming to DC this spring, I immediately thought of my two-year-old daughter, Evie, and her fear of bugs. I wanted a fun and lighthearted way to tell her what would soon be happening. I told my mom, Patsy, that I wished there were a book for young children to explain the phenomenon.

Thus, Cecily Cicada was born while we were on a road trip to visit my girls' cousins, Hannah and Addis. Evie and baby Lucy slept in the back while Mom and I collaborated in rhyme. My mom's illustrations brought humor and life to Cecily.

While Cecily's message of patience and hope is relevant to the seventeen-year cicada cycle, we realized it is a timeless message as well.

We hope you enjoy reading it as much as we enjoyed writing it.

Kita Helmetag Murdock
Patsy Helmetag
Spring 2004